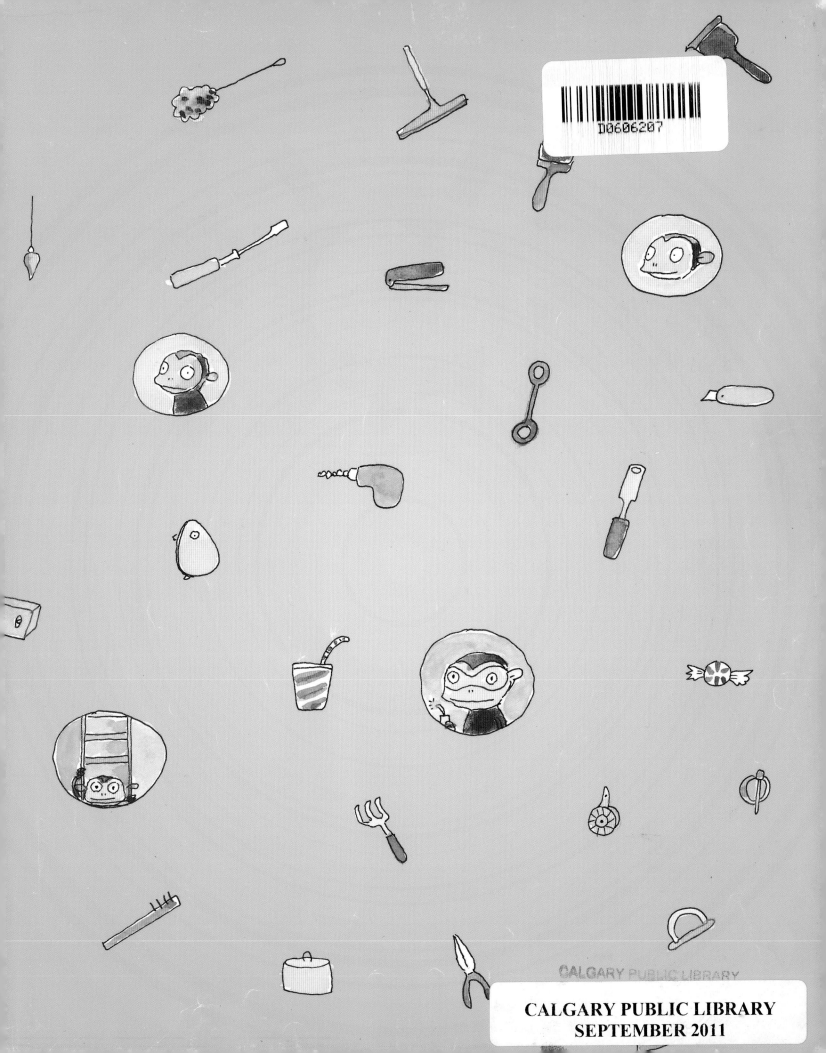

Monkey With A Tool Belt

and the SEASIDE SHENANIGANS

Chris Monroe

CAROLRHODA BOOKS MINNEAPOLIS

To Captain Dann —CM

Carolrhoda Books
A division of Lerner Publishing Group, Inc.
241 First Avenue North
Minneapolis, MN 55401 U.S.A.

Website address: www.lernerbooks.com

Library of Congress Cataloging-in-Publication Data

Monroe, Chris.
    Monkey with a tool belt and the seaside shenanigans / written and illustrated by Chris Monroe.
        p.   cm.
    Summary: Chico the clever monkey helps his friend Clark the elephant solve a problem at a seaside resort.
    ISBN: 978-0-7613-5616-5 (lib. bdg. : alk. paper)
    [1. Monkeys—Fiction. 2. Elephants—Fiction. 3. Repairing—Fiction. 4. Resorts—Fiction.] I. Title.
PZ7.M760Mor 2011
[E]—dc22   2011003013

Manufactured in the United States of America
1 — DP — 7/15/11

Chico Bon Bon was fixing a sprinkler on a hot summer day.

The sprinkler had been spraying too much water!

Then it stopped
spraying.

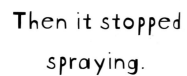

Chico took a
closer look.

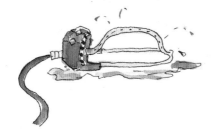

"This may require some fixing," he said.

Chico had all the tools for the job in a little tool box tucked in his tool belt.

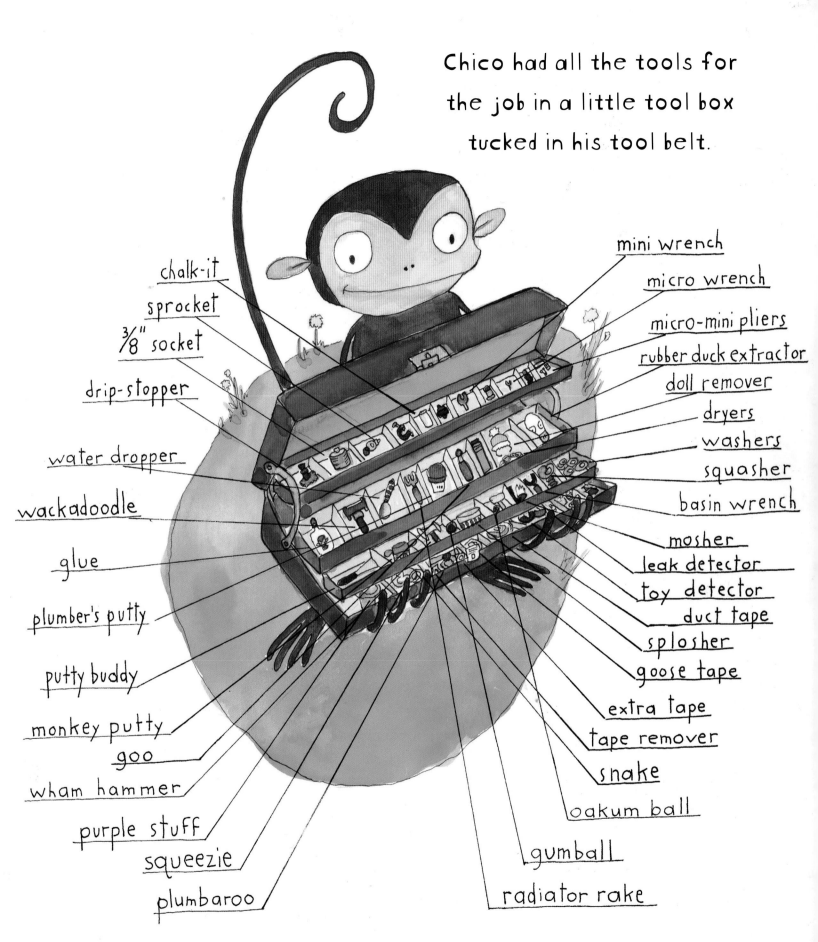

chalk-it
sprocket
3/8" socket
drip-stopper
water dropper
wackadoodle
glue
plumber's putty
putty buddy
monkey putty
goo
wham hammer
purple stuff
squeezie
plumbaroo

mini wrench
micro wrench
micro-mini pliers
rubber duck extractor
doll remover
dryers
washers
squasher
basin wrench
mosher
leak detector
toy detector
duct tape
splosher
goose tape
extra tape
tape remover
snake
oakum ball
gumball
radiator rake

The sprinkler was soon working again.

It was a postcard from Clark!

He was on vacation at his uncle's seaside resort.

The postcard read:

Editions Elephantique

33¢

Dear Chico,
Please come to the beach. We need your help at my uncle's resort. Things are breaking. Please come soon!

Your friend,
Clark

P.S. Also, we can go surfing! The waves here are sweet.

Chico Bon Bon
Big Tree House
Next to Elsa's

"I think I will go to the beach!" thought Chico Bon Bon. "They definitely need my help." Chico was also a big fan of SURFING.

He packed his bags and called for a ride. Off they went!

But they had a few problems along the road:

A tire on the rickshaw went flat and fell over.
Chico fixed it with air, spearmint gum, and some clover.

A frog on a bicycle
went in the ditch.
Chico rescued his
bike with balloons
and a hitch.

They stopped at a drive-in
to eat some burritos.
He fixed a torn screen to
keep out the mosquitos.

Their root beer dispenser
was having some trouble.
He loosened a nut . . . and out
popped a bubble!

Soon they arrived at the beach. The rickshaw driver said
good-bye and pedaled off. Chico looked around.

The resort looked amazing!

Clark came walking up the beach. He was wearing a Hawaiian shirt, Hawaiian shorts, and a Hawaiian visor. (He had forgotten his tool belt at home.)

Hey, Chico!! Am I ever glad to see YOU! Something is running amok here, and we don't know what it is!

Chico was glad to see his old friend, but his outfit made it a little hard to focus.

They walked down to one of the cabanas. It had a big hole in the roof.

Several coconuts and some popcorn were underneath the hole.

It looks like something... or someONE... fell through.

Chico put on his safety harness and climbed the roof.
He didn't see anything unusual except for a green
feather and a big piece of seaweed. He tucked the
feather in his tool belt. Then he
fixed the hole with some palm leaves,
twine, and nails.

The next broken thing was one of Uncle Bill's little sailboats.

Something had scuffed the floor so much that now the boat was leaking!

Whatever it was had also filled the sailboat's storage bench with bread crumbs!

"This is odd," thought Chico, as he carefully repaired the bottom of the boat. He patched it and then vacuumed up the bread crumbs with a wet-dry vac he borrowed from a friendly sea captain.

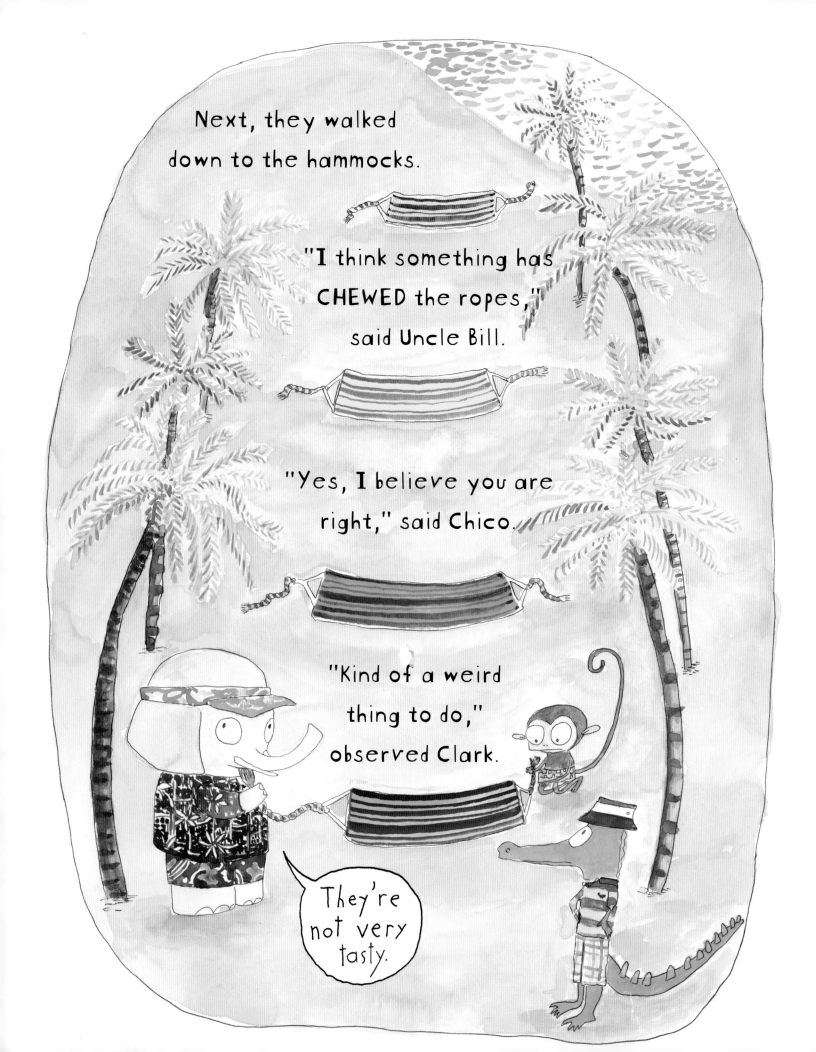

Chico repaired the ropes and retied the hammocks.

Underneath, he found a cupcake wrapper and triangular footprints in the sand.

Just then, one of the lifeguards ran up.

Something's wrong with the waterslide!

They all rushed to the slide.

The water was barely trickling down the tube!

Where's all the water?!!

Crawling out is hurting our knees!!

SWOOSH

Suddenly they all heard a loud **SWOOSH** at the
top of the tube. Sliders blasted out of the bottom
of the slide!!

They were all OK but EXTREMELY WATERLOGGED.
They scrambled out of the pool.

Water was spraying out the bottom of the slide like a giant fire hose.

Everyone ran for cover . . .

Chico went behind the slide to a small building.

① The door would not budge.

② He checked the doorknob with his 90-degree turn detector.

No turning was detected.

③ He loosened it with his half-inch loosey loo.

④ He put a wobble wedge under the knob.

⑤ He sprayed some invisible oil behind the wedge.

It was hard to tell how much to use.

⑥ He dusted the keyhole with bubble powder. Three tiny bubbles floated out.

A good sign.

⑦ He felt hungry, so he ate a banana.

⑧ He wiggled the doorknob, then turned it slowly. It made a small sound:

click

The door unlocked.

He slowly pushed it
open and peeked around
the edge.
He looked inside the
pump room.
He could not believe
his eyes.

A large green duck was tap-dancing on the pump handle.

Chico had not expected this.
After a moment, he politely said:

"I'm causing PROBLEMS?" said the duck.

"Yes," said Chico, "some mice just went
on the ride of their lives."

"Would it help if I got
down from here?"
asked the duck.

"Yes," said Chico as the duck
backflipped onto the floor.

Chico turned the handle to slow down the water as the duck moonwalked backward into a pile of buckets.

As Chico helped him up, he realized something.

He pulled the feather from his tool belt pocket and held it up to the duck.

He noticed several things about the duck that matched some of the other clues.

He looked at the duck's feet. They matched the shapes in the sand by the hammocks.

Chico had solved the mystery.

Just then Clark and Uncle Bill showed up .

"I think I've figured out how everything got broken," said Chico, glancing toward the duck. "But I'm pretty sure it was accidental."

"A duck? That's all?" said Clark. "I thought it was a monster or a wild animal."

"Well, he IS a little wild, actually," said Chico, "but he is also a really good dancer."

The duck danced outside and hopped on his bike. He rode off down the beach.

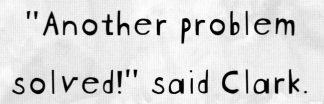

"Another problem solved!" said Clark.

You sure are good at fixing things, Chico.

I wonder if he'll come back? Well... at least everything is all fixed now.

So... guys... **now**, how about THIS idea?

So off they ran
to catch the last waves before sunset.

The end